CINDERELLA

and

the Furry Slippers

davide cali

raphaëlle barbanègre

tundra

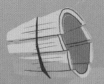

ONCE UPON A TIME there was a poor little girl named Cinderella who lived with a terrible stepmother and two even worse stepsisters.

She spent her days housecleaning while her awful stepmother and stepsisters had tea and cake.

Cinderella dreamed that one day an awesome prince on a white horse would come to save her. But no prince ever came; only more dishes to wash, floors to clean and hair to do.

The day of the annual prince's ball arrived.
Cinderella wanted to go, but she didn't have
a dress to wear.

So she secretly called a fairy godmother
to make an appointment.

Need help?
CALL NOW
514 ★ 806 ★ 0303

When the fairy godmother arrived, she wasn't quite what Cinderella had expected.

Are you sure this looks OK?

The fairy godmother's helpers didn't look like the animals in the ad.

And the dress didn't look like the picture from the magazine.

Don't worry, dear. You look beautiful!

The slippers were a little odd too.

Aren't they usually made of glass?

Glass? What a funny idea!

But worst of all was the coach.

And the horses? Let's not even mention those.

Cinderella arrived at the castle in her turnip.
The castle looked a little less grand than she
was expecting.

CASTLE

Inside, she found out about the dance contest.

The dancing was pretty weird.
And the prince wasn't even
paying attention.

Then it was Cinderella's turn.
Her dance was simply . . .

. . . the worst of all!

But when the prince woke up and noticed the girl with one shoe doing her strange dance, he immediately fell in love with her!

He picked Cinderella for
the solo dance. And when
he took her in his arms . . .

. . . Cinderella discovered that the prince was much better in the magazine.

What a disappointment! And the turnip
wasn't even there to bring her home.

She had just started the long walk back when something caught her eye.

And she lived happily ever after.

Published simultaneously in the United States of America by Tundra Books of Northern New York, an imprint of Penguin Random House Young Readers, a Penguin Random House Company

Library of Congress Control Number 201695779

Edited by Samantha Swenson
Designed by Five Seventeen
The artwork in this book was rendered digitally.
The text was set in Arrus and Folk.

Printed and bound in China

www.penguinrandomhouse.ca

1 2 3 4 5   21 20 19 18 17

Penguin
Random House
TUNDRA BOOKS

tundra

To Clément, all over again —RB

Library and Archives Canada Cataloguing in Publication

Calì, Davide, 1972–, author
    Cinderella and the furry slippers / Davide Calì ; illustrations by Raphaëlle Barbanègre.

Issued in print and electronic formats.—ISBN 978-1-101-91899-9 (epub)
ISBN 978-1-101-91898-2 (hardback).—ISBN 978-1-101-91899-9 (epub)

    I. Barbanègre, Raphaëlle, 1985–, illustrator II. Title.

PZ7.C1283Ci 2017   j823'.92   C2016-906707-6
                                        C2016-906708-4